Greta's Revenge

REVENGE

MORE ALICE AND GRETA

by Steven J. Simmons

illustrated by Cyd Moore

Dragonfly Books • Crown Publishers • New York

DRAGONFLY BOOKS® PUBLISHED BY CROWN PUBLISHERS

Text copyright © 1999 by Steven J. Simmons
Illustrations copyright © 1999 by Cyd Moore

Published by Crown Publishers, a division of Random House, Inc.,
1540 Broadway, New York, NY 10036

www.randomhouse.com/kids

Library of Congress Cataloging-in-Publication Data
Simmons, Steven J., 1946–
Greta's revenge : more Alice and Greta / by Steven J. Simmons ; illustrated by Cyd Moore.
p.   cm.
Summary: Greta, a witch who enjoys playing nasty tricks on people,
tries to make the kind witch Alice just like her, but the spell backfires.
I. Moore, Cyd, ill. II. Title.
PZ7.S59186Gr   1999
[Fic]—dc21
98-47074
ISBN 0-517-80051-9 (trade)
ISBN 0-375-80685-7 (pbk.)

First Dragonfly Books® edition: September 2000
Printed in the United States of America

10 9 8 7 6 5 4 3 2 1

But Alice had followed Greta. She waved her wand and said,

Whatever you chant, whatever you brew,
Sooner or later comes back to you!

Immediately, the bug juice disappeared from the playground and covered the ground where Greta was standing. Greta slipped and fell head over heels.

Alice mumbled to herself, "Poor Greta. When will she learn!?"

Later Alice said, "Let's go help some kids clean up their street." But Greta had had enough of helping. She flew to a school playground where she thought it would be fun to cover the monkey bars, rings, and swings with slippery bug juice and watch the children slip and slide. She waved her wand and cackled,

Squishy spiders, worms, and bees,
Slide these children to their knees!

The children started falling to the ground.

Alice and Greta flew to a family where they had heard there had been an outbreak of chicken pox. They wanted to clear up the children's itchy red spots. Together they waved their wands and chanted,

Alakazam, alakazeer, tiny red spots disappear!

The kids' mom looked in disbelief into the clear faces of her smiling children.

Within a few weeks, Greta got tired of doing bad things and asked Alice if she could help her for a day. Although Alice was surprised, she said, "Sure." And together they took off on their brooms.

I think I've been *Kind of nasty...*

In a little while, the spells on both witches wore off entirely. Alice's hat turned back to rosy pink. Greta's hat turned back to mean green. Each witch could remember what she had done under the spell, but ever so vaguely.

Alice scratched her head and said, "I think I've been kind of nasty, but I don't know why. I can't wait to help people. That always makes me feel great."

And Greta said, "I think I've been kind of good, but I'm not sure why. When I start doing nasty things, I'll feel better. But every once in a while, maybe I'll help that pathetic Alice."

I think I've been *Kind of good...*

On another day, Greta was handing out favorite baseball cards to some grateful boys and girls when she suddenly stopped and said to herself, "Oh, frogs' feet and lizards' guts—what am I doing!?" She turned every baseball card dark blue and laughed hysterically when the children started to cry.

But as time went by, the spells weakened. One very hot day, Alice was busy melting some children's ice cream and laughing as they cried. Suddenly, she stopped and mumbled to herself, "Goodness gracious, what am I doing!?" She quickly made each child a new ice cream pop with special candy topping and enjoyed watching smiles return to their faces.

Alakazam, alakazeer, make a tower reappear!

The blocks immediately went back into the shape
of a tower. The children could not believe their eyes.
They waved their thanks to Greta.

Next, Greta walked past some children who
had spent hours making a big building with blocks.
Just as they finished, their dog bumped into it and
the blocks fell all around him. As the children cried
out, Greta pointed her wand and quickly chanted,

A baby cloud appeared next to the cat and gently carried her down to the two children.

Greta immediately flew off in search of good things to do. She saw a brother and sister trying to help their cat, who was stuck up a tree. They were having terrible trouble since the tree was too tall for them to climb.

Greta waved her wand in circles over her head and whispered,

Bat wings up, bat wings down,
Let this cat float to the ground!

Greta had never learned the most important lesson at the Witch School that she and Alice had attended as young girls. Their teacher had called it the "Brewmerang Principle": "Whatever you chant, whatever you brew, sooner or later comes back to you!"

Greta then yelled something she had never, ever said before:

I want to do such fine, nice things!

Her magic was indeed coming back to her in a most unexpected way.

The next day, while Alice fed some lizards and toads, Greta played with her snakes and spiders. Suddenly, Greta began to feel very strange. Her body began to shake. She smiled at the butterflies and flowers. And then her yucky green hat turned bright pink.

Once at the picnic, they waved their wands
and chanted:

Bat wings up, bat wings down,
blow this picnic all around!

They both laughed as a strong wind blew the
food onto everyone's clothes. The children went
home hungry.

In the boiling potion, they saw the image of a picnic with children eating peanut butter and jelly sandwiches, pizza, fruit, and cookies.

Alice and Greta flew off together to do their dirty work.

The next morning, Greta joined Alice for a cup of pond slime. Together they stirred a cauldron and chanted,

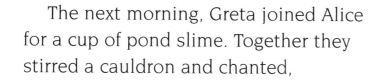

Time to brew, time to bubble,
time to stir up nasty trouble!

Greta laughed as she watched Alice fly off to a birthday party. There, the children were having so much fun as a clown made them balloons in the shape of animals. Alice waved her wand and chanted,

Spiders crawl, toads hop, bees sting, balloons pop!

With that, the balloons burst and changed into the real animals! The children's laughter turned into tears as they became frightened and ran away.

The watering can suddenly dropped from Alice's hand. Her body began to shake. Her beautiful pink hat turned yucky green. And then Alice's smile turned into a snarl, and she said words she had never, ever said before:

Oh, I want to do such nasty, nasty things!

The next day, Greta hid behind a rock watching Alice water her flowers. She then pointed her wand at Alice and whispered,

Stars, moon, sun, and sea,
make this witch become like me!

No, Greta thought, Alice deserves worse! And then she came up with a wonderfully bad idea. "I will make Alice just like me!" she cackled. "I will make that pink goody two-shoes do nasty things just like me! We can drink our morning cup of pond slime together and figure out our bad day's work!"

Greta wondered what she could do to get even with Alice. Maybe she would cover Alice in honey and let loose a hive of bees to fly around her. Greta would have such a good laugh at that!

Perhaps she would turn Alice's broom into a baseball bat. Alice would be so surprised when she flew into the branches of a tree. Greta smiled with delight!

Today Greta was angry with Alice. Alice had just spoiled one of Greta's devious schemes by putting her in an icky, sticky marshmallow mess.

Alice and Greta were witches with two very different views of the world. Alice used her magic to help people. Greta, on the other hand, used her spells to do things that were not very nice.

To Eileen, Sara, Caroline, Julia,
Nick, and Cliff, once again, with much love
—S.J.S.

For the free-spirited, and one and only,
truly original Lindsay Moore
—C.M.